Koker

ROOPLALL

MONAR

First published 1987
Peepal Tree Press
53, Grove Farm Crescent
Leeds LS16 6BZ
Yorkshire
England

ISBN 0 948833 05 X

Introduction

No writer has explored more persistently or more consciously
the state of being Indo-Caribbean than Rooplall Monar.
Others more celebrated, such as V.S.Naipaul in *A House For
Mr. Biswas*, Ismith Khan in *The Jumbie Bird* and Shiva Naipaul in
Fireflies and *The Chip-Chip Gatherers*, have given moving and
exact accounts of the break-up of the ancestral world-views
and cultural practices which Hindus and Muslims living in
Trinidad and Guyana maintained with some degree of
wholeness up to the 1940s. Each of those novels leaves its
characters in a state of limbo, in between a disappearing past
and an uncertain future, reluctant to enter the Creole world of
the Caribbean. Each of those writers left the Caribbean in their
early adult lives; Rooplall Monar has stayed, and one can see it
as both a matter of biography and vision, that he should have
gone beyond seeing the state of 'limbo' as an unimaginable
void and expressed in his poetry what Wilson Harris meant
when he talked of *Limbo* as reflecting 'a certain kind of gateway
or threshold to a new world and the dislocation of a chain of
miles.' (*History, Fable and Myth in the Caribbean and Guianas* 1970)
Monar sees both the pain and the possibilities in the state of
limbo, the new juncture and the tension implied in the title
Indo-Caribbean.

The crisis, of personal psyche and cultural orientation, is
summed up in Monar's question

> O who am I
> between a dying consciousness
> a growing vision

Monar writes out a conflict between an ancestral consciousness
which he can never really declare is dead, and an Indo-
Guyanese vision which he can never be sure has real roots.
There is an ever-present awareness of the specific history of the
Indo-Guyanese worker's oppression as an indentured
labourer and even as a 'free' labourer on the sugar estates. In
poems such as 'Drought' he wonders how that experience can
ever be owned. There is also a constant tension between the
conviction that the ancestral traditions are dead and the

awareness that:

> Ancestral blood still seeps in my veins
> generations...
> generations of gods cloud my eyes

The tentative movement out of this state of limbo is sought in several directions. One is a general search for sources of consolatory meaning in the stark history of Guyanese slavery, explored in such poems as 'The Chimney At Chateau Margot' and 'Patterns'. A second is in the embracing of what Monar sees as the beginnings of a native tradition, albeit a broken one, in the unique self-created 'bung coolie' culture of the sugar estate communities which Monar described realistically in his *Backdam People: A Collection of Short Stories* (1985). This world is conveyed through the images of the estate landscape of punts, tarred bridges, watch houses and greenheart culverts. The third source of meanings is sought in local traditions of spiritual resistance to what Monar sees as the ossifications of brahminical Hinduism, a resistance expressed in the mixing of the South Indian traditions of *bhakti* and the proletarian and sometimes anti-brahminical ideology of the estate worker. 'Coming Of The Rain' explores this iconoclastic tradition.

However, there is no easy arrival at a sense of possibility. Tension is the true state of Monar's poetry. This is both a psychic tension between spiritual hope and despair and a social tension between a deep commitment to Guyana and a bitter anger at the state of Guyanese society after twenty years of independence. The last ten poems in the collection confront a society which has been brought to the edge of 'the mutilation of the spirit' that Monar writes about in 'Fear'. Beyond these political statements is a cosmic sense of anguish, a sense of inescapable ambivalence which Monar explores in the profound, complex and multi-layered title poem of the collection: 'Koker'. Here the cultural tensions between ancestral voices and the difficult commitment to an Indo-Guyanese beginning are but one level of a tormented sense of division between the urge to be part of the cycle of creation and the urge to escape from it. The koker, the Dutch device for controlling the flow of water in and out of the sugar estate, is a perfect image for the boundary point at which Rooplall Monar conducts his deeply felt exploration of the Indo-Caribbean condition.

Jeremy Poynting

Contents

Creole Gang

Baling and throwing
among green canes from rusty punts,
their sweated faces
show how many days and nights have passed
between cane roots and black streams,
sunburnt trashes and parched earth,
wearied days and restless reality.
Their hands and limbs are but fragments
that walk and bathe,
when sun shines, rains fall
and drivers shout.
Who can tell when midday meets
their rest - they eat, they talk?
Their limbs cry and hearts burn.
Is this not the century of dreams,
of tales told by ancestors
of a faith told by life?
Again and again they will bale and throw
curse and rest among green canes
and black earth, wishing, wishing...

The Chimney At Chateau Margot

It began in antique ingenuity
like the pyramids
paging the histories of generations
in an alien land.
It stands unconquered
defying times saddened moments,
its form patiently mortared
by hands which lived for release
on beds of straw,
dreaming of a messiah
in apocalyptic hope.

As Dutch masters ravished black virgins
awaiting the next arrival of the fleet
to ship hogs-heads and rum,
as Quamina brooded in anger,
as John Smith, consoled only with a Bible
and another tomorrow,
clawed death in triumph,
these tired goldsmiths
costumed the colossus.

Each stone placed in perfection's image
they walled themselves to create history
as blood and tears mettled this monument
that now towers three centuries old
brooding upon the builders it has slain.

Patterns

Here at Chateau Margot
things lie in sleep
breathing in chorus
butchered tales
of slaves who cried out
under the sun;
of moonlit lovers
dusted in an affinity
with sugar and whips.

Wandering spirits now beckon me
to mouldered stones
whose silence hatches meanings
as leaves decay into colours
thrilling the spirit,
to birds perched on over-grown pathways,
black-eyed crows, ravishing
heaps of rotted mangoes,
begetting new blossoms,
though the climber falls
consumed by the tree

Patterns like leaves
blown by the wind
for more patterns to pattern.
Patterns are forever here
like a storm
rising in fury,
fishing Dageraad,
Kyk Over Al, Fort Nassau,
then dying with immortal wound
until waves climax on the beach
assuring the fisherman of a catch.

Going For Lawah

Two haggard old men
torn by seasons and cane scorpions
beat in pained ecstasy
the Lawah drums.

They go singing
these bangled women,
daughters of jehaji's desecration
happy for the wedding
of Ramesh and Savitri,
who, though yet children,
question their altars
knowing their gods are polluted.

Their wombs of fertility
are caressed by other spirits,
for the drums,
native of far-away shores,
are reluctant to vibrate in them
passions of birth:
marriage is not yet theirs.

The Brahmin Girl

You look at me with scorn,
still I cherish my love for you,
not like your father
kneeling before his clay gods
calling the sun in another voice,
ignorant of pregnant baboons
in mukku-mukku bush
this rainy August.

Here is life and love
already to fertilize,
bending paddy sheaves in moonlight
if my arms clasp yours.

In my kingdom
mantras and flowered gods
have no place
but what's received at payday.
Look, night beetles dance
round bottle lamps,
villagers, done counting their
shillings and half-bits,
love in the sweet smell of the canefields.
On their brows, in women's wombs
germinates a dream of cities,
new heritage, undying statues.

Brahmin girl, don't you know your womb
is a vacuum if not lipped in sugar canes.
Like your father
whose existence alternates
between temples and ceremonies
you'll die in a dream
of Ramayan, mantras, lores.

Can't you feel between your thighs
touch of birth, hunger for caress,
thirst for motherhood,
O Brahmin girl.

Babu

Huddled by the front door
of a decayed, rat-infested logie,
victim of rain and sun,
Babu's eyes scan the canefield horizons.

Whiplash explodes from sunburnt hands
leering blue eyes in hardened faces
a jingling of copper coins
a dumb powerless deity
dancing a dance of images

images of immigrant ships
barrack confinements
cutlasses, decapitated women
dance in the rhythm of seasons

an enclosed world of canefields
waves of spluttering factory smoke
days of rotating nothingness

In a heave of impatience
Babu swirls like a ballet dancer
strong and flexible:

Generations nurtured from my seeds
will clasp their hands and say
our ancestors carved those fields
which have given us meanings
meanings to stand tall

This land is ours.

Moongaza

Two a'clack ah manin
moonlight shine
daag bark
Bow wow wow
fram de ole loco-line.

Look fram yuh kitchin winda
O Gaad neighba! Moongaza!
lang like coc'nut tree
wid lang silva haan
red red red eye

O Gaad me fraid!
'E foot wide open
gazin at de moon in de canefiel'

Mule-bye run fuh he life.
Duck!
'Low Moongaza pass quick quick
fuh do e bizness
wid Massa in de berrin-grung

Memba granmudda dem peep
Moongaza in dem logie
when 'e do bizness wid Massa
an' dem fraid! fraid! fraid!
Neighba Stella picknie
dead blue in she belly
cause she see Moongaza
same night dem fowl cack crow
cook coo roo roo.

Memba watchman Djoko?
Drop. Stone dead.
'E mule tramp 'e,
kick 'e,
mash 'e,
cause 'e tek tree shade foh Moongaza.

Memba 'hole nigga yaad
sleep soon
when ole folk
see Moongaza in de canefiel'?

Me skin raise big!
Ow Moongaza! Moon... Ga... Za!
me picknie! me picknie!

Cook coo roo roo
Moongaza done 'e bizness
Bow wow wow
'E leave de estate foh bad

O Gaad neighba, Lawd!
Moongaza mouth wid blood.

Ahwe picknie, ahwe picknie
Moongaza squeeze am out
yuh life
foh Massa in e grave!
Moongaza squeeze am out yuh life
foh Massa in c grave
Ahwe picknie... ahwe picknie.

Ko-Ko Moore (B.A.)

Now Ko-Ko Moore a gone an' dead
Who doctah jumbie in we head?
Fadda have mercy on him soul!

Him was de best obeah man
From country village up to town
who fix you prappa good an strong
with 'e breath an 'e sound,
he occult parphanalia
an de holy-holy water.

Now poor him a gone and dead
With all he obeah in he head
an was not one ahwe pay respec'
or tear-drop lilbit dry-cry self
so him soul could rest in peace.

But yuh rememba Ko-Ko Moore?
Praise be de Lord!
Bachelor of all Black Art?

Yuh rememba de sunny day
Pon de shell-bank seashore
when he lash-out de jumbie
outa Maacoon madee-madee head
den t'row way de cane-whip an clip-hair
in de sea-bed an say:
'Begone yuh vile devil, begone...'

O Heavenly fadda dat was a day...
De tapoo-drum been beating racka-tay racka-tay
While half-naked women singin and dancin
and two-three devotee saying:
'Bless dis day O mudda Durga, bless dis day...'

18

While Ko-Ko in a voice like thunder say:
'I command yuh, O I command yuh...'

Yuh rememba grandmudda Ismay
who shakin-hip in village to this day?
O Christ Jesus, she 'hole foot gat chigga
An was na docta coulda cure dat nigga
'Cept Ko-Ko Moore who been skill an prappa
fo bush medicine dem toes get betta
now Grandmudda Ismay young as eva!

An what of Tantie Alice who had bucketful a' trouble
with she sweet man in Buxton front
Who na tink that she was more dan skunt
cause he only sleepin with she
every kiss-me-ass night
As if she is one common 'hore
an when Sat'day come
He ain't want pay-up de score
but he in de rum-shop firing rum...
Till one night Alice rap-tap-tap
pon Ko-Ko Moore front door
an cry-up an say she proppa sore
an Uncle Ko-Ko Moore
must get this Buxton sweetman fo she
Else she, Alice, is no tru woman
An Ko-Ko Moore no good obeah man

An nex' night Ko-Ko Moore a tell she:
'Me obeah conqua science-medicine
an me powda mek one jumbie-ghost
come long long like lantern post...
Now me, Ko-Ko Moore, truly give yuh
dis obeah powda
which yuh must sprinkle in him metemgee
an if you, Alice, ain't get him fo good
when yuh wear dis charmulet

den Ko-Ko Moore ain't sound an fit
to practice bush an keep obeah-kit.'

An compay! when one month gone in de calendar
Ko-Ko Moore word come tru as eva
cause Alice been done hear de ban,
in front de pulpit hug de Buxton man,
An when the pastor pronounce dem man an wife
Den Alice say, she inside come to life,
'Praise be to Ko-Ko Moore, O Lord, praise be...'

An when Barney been playin jumbie
an whole village been come to see
how he fraff'n-up an talkin many a tongue
an actin like he head ain't sound,
eh-eh! na ah Ko-Ko Moore they consult
cause it had to do with de occult?

An memba bin one dark midnight
an not a livin soul in sight
'cept Ko-Ko Moore an dis Barney
unda Komaka tree in a pentagram-circle
An when Barney start playin jumbie-jumbie
Ko-Ko Moore grab him an say:
'In de name a' Jesus an Maha Kali
release dis prisoner now or neva
else me Ko-Ko Moore put yuh in grave for eva.
Release dis man I orda yuh
else Ko-Ko Moore's no obeah man fo true.

An nex four-five day Barney lookin good an sound
when everybody spottin him around
and when they see him dancin at the cumfa
they say Ko-Ko truly mend him proppa.

But now Ko-Ko Moore gone an dead dead dead
Stab one night by Miriam pon he bed,
de village 'hore who bin get typee for he,
so she de want him fo sheself fo sure
cause plenty women bin love Ko-Ko Moore.

But now Ko-Ko Moore ah dead an gone
O Lord have mercy on him bones
O fadda may him rest in peace
Peace unto him O fadda.

Darling Of The Rising Sun

I see your sacred lotus lips
and I know the chant in your heart
I see your tall tresses dancing in the wind
and I know the longings in your soul
as you do homage to the godhead of the rising
sun

How I wish, O female devotee
to sanctify that barren ova of your maidenhood,
woman of dark illusions
in this our dispossessed but pregnant world

Why pour your life's affection
like silver raindrops on a sterile image
to a god far away,
a dumb god once buried
in your grandfather's copper trunk,
a god whose potency reigns
in red bamboo flags flying in your yard

I long to fertilize your womb
begetter of many sons -
to baptize you with brown soil
staining my hands
in the hour of twilight,
the hour of creation

I long to sacrifice that clay god
and shape you in the likeness
of my own god of the canefields and ricefields

Don't you know the lineaments of my ancestry,
the cane-ashed streams
now flowing in my blood,
the wounds in my blood,
the riotous rage in my veins,
swollen like full forest rivers.

I think you understand,
Darling of the rising sun,
the symbol of my shrine.

Situations

You came storming into my life
poor lonely Monza
without knowing who I am

Will you give what I craved
through years, schooling myself
into canefields and greenheart culverts
knowing nothing else?

When you came into my life
neither the beauty of a savannah sunset
nor the raptures of the night beetles
could slake my thirst.

Then I think
how harsh is life
that we are dying slowly
to enrich the womb
that sunset and the bees will remain
when we are dust, yet even so
out of us may come other lives
to glory in sunset and beetles.

I, (who knows?) who might have,
under your inspiration,
been one with sunset and savannahs
together exploring watch-houses and punt-trenches,
let me not think too much
squandering the present on a dream
and with it lose you too
and die a penitent man.

Meanings

One handful of ploughed earth
gives me communion
with clouds, mossy streams,
flooded canals.

Not of illusions
nor cries
that fruited these canefields
infested with white scorpions
nor of that far horizon

I am encompassed in midday heat
colliding punts, tarred bridges.
I am now life-in-death
stripped of a shaming consciousness
of my predicament,
languishing in the worlds of watch-house,
endless streams,
greenheart culverts.

Let not the sun move westwards
nor my heart beat
though the factory bell rings
for evening hours are painful
as night descends over the plantation
breaking this communion
which is so sweet
so endless
so consciousless.

Why should withered gods mock me
now that I have forgotten the past
insensible to the present
becoming as they wished

one with high bridges
patient mules
black streams?

Why should night disturb my sleep
making me yet conscious of that horizon,
the humiliation
and the agony?

Tonight I pray for rain to fall
silencing crickets and frogs
from across the fields,
not wanting to hear other voices
but welcoming morning
returning me to canefields, deep savannahs

I sit in the watch-houses,
not in a temple seeking alien deity,
while still water runs to cane fields
Here I will seed my crops
after a sacrificial feast
budding virginity for meanings
in thrilling ecstasy of nakedness
Here, where generations sleep,
in the canefields fed
from calabashes of wounded pride
'...Hassan dead dead dead...O Hassan dead.'

This agony stirs in me a memory
making me primitive
Seeking a resurrection
let me hug that culvert
let the water bathe me
let me commune with flooded canefields
pregnant clouds, tarred bridges

meanings are born here
meanings are born here

Limbo

Ancestral blood still seeps in my veins
Generations of gods cloud my eyes
How will ripe cane-arrows
bring life to my logie?
Will I ever unravel
the circles of my riddle?

Who am I
between buried copper trunks
voices in the cemeteries?
O who am I
between a dying consciousness,
a growing vision?

Were my great great grandfather's lean brown hands
chained eternally round jointed stems of night and
day,
his loins spanning barren lands
for his dynasty of sons?
My nannie's sagging breast
cruelly devoured by eyes of another harsh world
so cruel between the immovable sun
and the ever-present cane scorpions?
And waves drowning winds in our ears?
and waves forever carrying perplexed tales
deceiving my great grandfather?

Now remains in the movement of my mind
an inexplicable limbo
horizons of silence and indecision
black birds flapping on the roofs of my sleep
strange secrets all around
strange sun and wind and rain
such strange and unwelcoming welcome.

Who am I to suffer this infinite agony
this vessel of coined-veins
Who am I?
Perhaps there will be a flood
for dying is the beginning of our birth,
death the beginning of my great grandfather's
dynasty of sons.

Drought

I still am being plagued:
so long coloured suns settle the sky
so long white scorpions contaminate
my breath

Leaves are all dried
ashed by lazy winds
to dry ponds
of scattered fish-bones
in ragged mounds.

I still am being plagued
divided by horizon's edges, yet
telling me of no other worlds
but mine,
my hut on this Mazaruni's bank,
yet pregnant with the voice in me
which stretches fleetingly
to the beyond.

I know crops will be here
right here on the river bank
when grieving hands
have burnt the pyre
the bank cleansed by carrion crows
when, after affinity with the bride,
meanings are created at
the pendant breast.

But I am still stifling
in this drought.
Something weighs my hands
and owls cry in the dark
remembering incestuous cohabitation.

But meanings are grown
between sensations of the thighs
between love and passion
between war and peace.

A strong wind now circles the night
the rain beats in passion
then thunder roars
killing coloured suns and white scorpions

And all are washed
for the birth.
She,
my alien wife, will die
for my origin is found,
my meanings -

but I am dead.

Let the child nourish itself
for paps of paddy line its cradle
tall, tall sugar canes greet the eye.

Metamorphosis

I walk wearily in barren fields
not a root giving sap to my sterility
sun-burnt peasants still tend their cows
fanatic saddhus still stare at the morning sun
as I dream of moonlit fish on the beach

How many stars have poisoned my lineage?
How many bear witness that
once I drowned between sea beds -
who could wish a better death
than live with this curse on their forehead?

Not even a grain of paddy
crowning the palm of my hands,
not even a woman
soothing my contorted shadow

I remember the boat of my youth
the laurels of marble-playing.
Will the palm of my hands
cup the coin of salvation?
Must I resurrect for a second birth
the wicked serpent again,
for Shiv's dances enchant the Cobra?
Can our death beget our birth?

Snake Altar

My forsaken god of the snake altar
my brown god, your very smile
betrays the blood in my veins.
Yet strange sacrifices are still heaped on your
shrine
re-invoking your make-believe presence.

God of another horizon
You are dead to me
dead like a stone.
But little children have lost faith
in the procreative ceremonies of the cane fields.
More worlds are marching
like a barbarous Spanish horde
on the virgin Guyana shores

O God, I need more water
in this barren kingdom
more water to sap the roots of my paddy
Where are the fruits of our meanings?

My Neighbour's Castle

Whom do I wrong
in my neighbour's castle?
Whom?

Voices mock me like winds
playing ballet with a fisherman's net
as the strong waves lash the shore

Walking the streets I see
betrayed faces already smeared
by history's mad encounters

Like a lost sentinel I watch
while the world sleeps
while I watch this jungle of destruction

Why did Columbus live?
Could I not die in the sanctum
of my mother's womb?

How I detest this blood in my heart,
yet sickness knows its victims
and claims them like a lover

Had the world been upside-down
would I fear the beat of my heart?

Ishwar

But Ishwar
why such silence?
My hands are far from yours?
My lips echo your name
in reverence.

Have you seen,
my Ishwar,
the curse on this land
lusting on innocence
ravaging dreams carved from
my Matha's womb?

Have you seen
clouds darkened by strange signs
awaiting chances for a drink?

O Ishwar
reveal to me
the origin of my birth

Plants are mothered
so are birds and flowers
gems of a day's delight
but not I.

Many seasons, births and deaths
pass like the wind
yet I continue searching for my mother.
Is she dead?

My God, My Ishwar
save me before I am lost.
Let my children know
the purpose of my death
if not my birth
my Ishwar.

Coming Of The Rain

Yesterday, cracked contours of silence
a ring of drought and nightmares,
rings of prayers, scarred hands imploring infinity
the god of this village temple
asleep in a dumb conclave.

Who dare wake these dying temple frescoes
and disturb the silence of long yesterday?

Once, these frescoes were the gods
as white-clad pundits scoured the altars
for devotees' offerings,
smiling that smile of deceit
and misinterpreting the Ramayan
to entranced followers,
lost souls, O myself, myself!

My seasoned pupils would be married
to cane roots
but without rain to fill the streams,
rain to grow my rice,
seeing the upright sun flame savannahs
in heaps of fire,
choked cattle round dry hoof-marked ponds
in this expanse of heat and repentence
I see death in the leaves of the tree
in the worms of the earth I see my death.

II

Boom!
Mortal peasants tear the temple gods to pieces
bony hands challenge the omnipotence of the sky
Boom, boom!
With opened eyes men become gods.

III

The drum of life throbs with passion
under the Dutch fig tree
hands are born from visions of death
hands palm the secrets of life
Krishna sees humble peasants
clutching statues of infinity
Krishna sees and knows and wills

IV

There is a wedding in the village
A wedding?

This day is meant for a ceremony
of man and gods
for only the eyes need rain
only the eyes

Birth

I am a stranger
among kumaka trees and black streams
scorching sun and angry rain.
I know no god from that ocean
who listens to me
in case I should pollute an ancient pride.
Here I am split by a past
that now manifests as a dream
reminding me with shame,
'I am not of here...'

Frail winds drum my ears,
a brand of lightening flashes,
yet I am unable to understand
Shiv's cyclic dances,
stifling procreation's ambition.
The lightening flashes
rooting my hut in a pool of rain
'O Bhagavan Bhagavan!'

My grandmother's raped cry re-echoes,
a vision of lashes on bare backs,
virgin breast exposed for white gods,
another flash of lightening,
more rain in graves of darkness.
'O God I am falling, falling, falling...'

Paralysed hands grasp for music
in the sanctum of sorrow
as Shiv's dances make confused
patterns with penis and clitoris
until original
original birth appears.

II

Watching a stream ripple
my imagination stretches back,
but I am unable to remember.

A cow in the pasture
runs
certain of her pen,
runs,
for a blade of grass
swaying in the winds.
She moos with pride.
Tears settle in the eye.

Koker

Belly waves roll upon waves
climbing on top the other
as unfulfilled lovers do
tumbling in whirlpools
at the end of desire,
then come splashing me in the face
drunk with the power of temporal grace.

But who knows
who ever knows the beginning of this dual agony?

I still wonder why the endurance
of sun-cracked weather,
silent carrion-crow clouds
white unending unending distance

Sometimes I question the origin of my birth
and the riddle of the proverbs:
who first saw the maker of this life,
or heard the first cry of creation?

I bear like pregnant paddy sheaves
everlasting burden of three months' rain
savannah surging waters.

They come, lost little children
seeking my age-old counsel.

I turn to myself and ponder
'Perhaps I am life-and-death -
yet I am neither
for unseeming tapestries weave
and weave...'

Out there in the ocean
something silently speaks with me
and only the wink of my eyes understand:
Am I sun or rain?
Am I godmother
to crabs, shrubs, courida?

Still they come
children of a lost land
into crevices of my worn-out body,
listening to that age-old dirge
afraid of the flood

Another worthless death -
for what?

I long to have the Atlantic winds
turn my wings
begin again the patterns of my life.
I hunger for the voices of the oceans,
fishing boats by my pillars
stars of the night

But do I serve
Man or Gods?

For I am neither life nor death,
drowned in age and ceremonies,
eyes for ever in question:
symbols
estrangement
seasons

On this curved punt bridge
I watch wrinkled black waters

sail away into eyeless savannahs
where sleep embryonic chinks
of a rebirth

This lonely watch-house by the bridge
reminds me of past love,
undying midday caresses -
my soul breaks into ripples
like a lump of dry earth
falling in a cool clear creek.

Sometimes my stunted bones crack
like burning bamboo joints
in the hot scorpion sun
as I remember the ordeal of
a twin baptism,
a twin consciousness

In dew-wet mornings
when crouching baboons listen half-asleep
and streaks of rain-smoke
settle on edges of limp canes,
I feel an unutterable joy,
a desire to clasp this horizon in my palms
becoming God and Man of these fields,
but past footprints,
shadows of a barbarous ritual,
follow me like an epileptic fit
whenever the first mule-whip crack,
breaks the morning silence.

In distant clouds
tales turn within the seasons
and sprinkling drops of rain
bless the sacrifice
when carrion crows are crowned
at ceremonies of another death-in-birth

I die many times in my sleep
in the mornings
I am old, old and strange
with a mind-telling agony
without origins
yet deep and meaningful

Yet how many times I totter
clutching impotent gods?
Succumb to these brutish
umbilical cords?
Among ruins and copper trunks
a voice forever wails
with the rushing winds.

II

Tides of rain and thunder
carved lines on my forehead,
my hard-corned palms
keep secrets of the soil
and courses of the winds.
Yet I am unable to decipher parables
of myself.

Here fields, savannahs, paddy sheaves
and the profile of myself
in the reflection of the stream:
A new day! a new day!
Signs of the marriage of many horizons
in these fields.

Judgement Day

Plants shrivelled
earth parched
rats and roaches
  inhabit the water pipe
so long it has been dry

In the socket of the eye
is an emptiness.
Is this our judgement day?

Is This The Temple?

Is this the temple where the jasmine
in the door-yard infused a godly quiet?
Where the blackwater pond,
its lilies fresh and blooming,
tempted fingers to the water,
tips of fingers to sanctify the forehead?
Where the deities were garlanded
in the temple's outer sanctum
on a filigreed wooden pedestal?
Where travellers found haven,
Where one lotus offered on the altar
was a marriage, a continuity:
the sugarcane fields, the factory smoke,
the peepal tree, images
of self-renewal.
The entrance is diverted,
jasmine shrivelled, pond muddied,
the deities cracked and crusted.
Worshippers tread the pathway,
their eyes sockets of mirage,
trying to comprehend,
but the sun dulls their perceptions
and helmeted, armed men
disenfranchise their reasoning.
The chain of continuity is snapped.

Mockery

Beyond the village junction
a half-filled stream
sandwiched with carrion-crow bush

Mangy dogs war round a bloated corpse;
the lifeless chimney, useless sluicegate
stand sentinel by forced mechanised crops.

The bumpy red-brick road meanders,
once like a woman's belly pregnant with countless
feet,
the legion of cutlass and shovel
their destiny carried on their foreheads

But who knows the whim of the gods?
False prophets deceived the eyes
their hands filled with ripe juicy fruits

The chimney
the sluice-gate
mock us all

Fear

It isn't the fear of death
but the mutilation of the spirit
that gnaws the mind,
dulls the senses into imbecility
shows the image of brutal man
in a cracked mirror

It is a mind habituated to fear -
a false turn quickens the pulses
a shadow's elongation
and the stomach retches;
a lonely moonlit night,
your wife and daughters
are bandits' playthings.

Breath is stifled
speech is muffled
limbs are paralysed

The eyes in the mirror
return your stare.

Was A Time

Was a time when you tramped
the city carefree
called the streets your own,

Was a time when you lorded
the brothels and cookshops
forded the streets and alleyways
like a prospector
jumping mounds in a river,
women swooning to cradle
your native body,
an image of brown earth and burnt sugarcane.

Was a time when,
oblivious of heat,
you rolled the crisp dollar bills between your
fingers
and a world of silk and perfume
greeted your tempted eyes.

Was a time when your hair well groomed,
nails polished, skin smooth,
shaped in tailored clothes,
the stomach feasted at every shop.

Was a time in this city
when, like a bird ruling the heavens,
growing up was innocence,
no thought of gunman's bullet,
nor helmeted sentry lurking in the streets,
no listening to every footfall,
the heartbeat reverberating in the ears.

No brothel-owner eyed you
as though you had escaped from jail
not daring to return your greeting

Was a time when freedom
enlarged your shadows
your feet planted in the city
seeds your ancestors have sown.

Was a time
was a time

Two Horizons

Had I known I would never have nurtured my
dreams
for a marriage in this village,
for a seed planted by countless scarred hands
germinating into the plant of fulfilment.

True, the faces in this village
were perplexed by riddles,
their eyes peering into the distance
   trying to decipher the wooden koker
where once tall sugarcanes loomed
nourished by hands and feet
whose destiny, merged with blood and earth,
had niched a half-clay god,
one step, two steps haltingly forward.

No more the villagers throng the backdam
for mango trees sprouting blossoms and fruits,
mouths relishing the succulent juices.
Men, anxious like solitary rats
scour the dead stumps, putrid leaves,
their throats parched, stomachs distended.

Hoofmarks dot the pasture
fishes in the stream bloat and stink
as the sun ascends the heavens

Old men in the village rub their scraggy faces:
is this plague descended through
the self-styled Pharoah,
reminding of a sister's warning years ago?

Will God intervene with another miracle
warning the Pharoah there is but one God?
Can we loosen the chains of self-imposed slavery
shackling this village
since Pharoah rigged the rod of authority?

Had I known men would have
metamorphosed into ghosts
stalking this village for roots and worms,
their reasons blinded by hunger
their fingers oozing blood
from the slaughter of a rash intruding brother
I would have sought a different horizon
though troubled in my sleep
by this dichotomy of two horizons.

In The Kingdom Of The Roach

I would never have believed
a man could become a boy
in four years
eyes baffled by empty shelves

Yet our footsteps are cautious
lest we trample the swarm of roaches
made sluggish by excess
fearful of arousing their arrogant claws

I would never have believed
how the streets forked
into cataleptic slums
in the kingdom of the roach

Passport

She scrounges the market
a lone carrion rummaging
a silent, grass-stunted pasture
searching the barren stalls
daring the challenge of emaciated sellers
their eyes flitting among the housewives.
Arms akimbo
empty basket slung on shoulder
dollar bills sticking to her fingers,
Sweat pours between breasts
murder would once have been committed
to pillow on, now shrunk
like sun-dried mangoes;
her long black hair,
net of so many admirers, turns grey;
lips which belched passion
fester at the corners.
She leaves the market
forlorn cat stoned from a yard
thinking of husband and children,
dreaming of a passport signifying salvation
faraway where the sky touches the ocean.

Will Tomorrow Bring Rain

Minute hands moving on the wall clock
chart the fear that creeps slowly
clustering like night-beetles on the lampshade.

Huddled in a half-lit bedroom
the sound of a distant footfall
smothers the scent of flowers.

Bodies crouched together,
perspiration drenched, stomachs soured,
a vision of bandits, cutlasses and guns.

Many have been mutilated of long straight hair,
their sleep haunted by nightmares:
decapitation, blood, rape.

This land lies like a corpse,
here an exhibition of ribs,
there the pulsing of exposed entrails,

while in distant towers
surfeited and sensual spiders
spin webs of intrigue and bloodshed.

This land is in eclipse.
Will tomorrow bring rain?

Notes

p.10 The Chimney At Chateau Margot - an old sugar estate factory chimney on the East Coast Demerara. Quamina - a deacon in the church of John Smith, Quamina lead the slave insurrection at Le Resouvenir in 1823 and was executed in its aftermath.
John Smith - the 'Demerara Martyr', a Methodist missionary who was found guilty of involvement in the Le Resouvenir rising, sentenced to death, reprieved by the British Government, but died in prison of consumption.
p.11 Dageraad, Kyk over Al, Fort Nassau - sites of the Berbice slave rebellion of 1763.
p.12 lawah - part of the wedding ceremony which, with the exception of male drummers, involves only women.
jehaji- shipmate, alludes to the shared voyage as indentured labourers.
p.15 Moongazer - a tall spirit which straddles roads, gazing at the moon, which devours people who try to pass under its legs.
p.17 mudda Durga - Mother Durga, one of the manifestations of Kali Mai, the black goddess of terrifying aspect who destroys evil through evil.
p.20 grandfather's copper trunk - sometimes the sole piece of personal furniture in the immigrants' logies, in which was held savings and precious possessions brought from India.
p.20 red bamboo flags - jandhi flags- erected to show a puja, or prayer ceremony has been held.
p.24 Hassan dead dead dead - the cry of mourning at the hossay or mohurrum festival for the slain martyrs, Hassan and Hussain; also perhaps an allusion to the death of Hassan in Wilson Harris's novel *The Far Journey of Oudin*.
p.25 logie - single-storey barracks housing for estate labourers.

p.29 Shiv's dances enchant the cobra - allusion to Shiva, the snake-armed, ithyphallic god whose dance makes the cycle of creation continue.

p.32 Ishwar - God, in the dualistic theology of Ramanuja.

p.34 Krishna - the avatar, incarnation of the god Vishnu.

p.35 Bhagavan - Bhagwan, the supreme being.

p.37 Koker - a sluice gate which controls the flow of water in and out of a sugar estate. At the front of the polder it keeps out the sea-water and at the back controls the amount of fresh water let in from the savannah.

p.37 the riddle of the proverbs:who first saw the maker of this life - Monar appears to allude to the Creation Hymn (Nasadiya) of the *Rig Veda* which begins:

> There was neither non-existence nor existence then; there was neither the realm of space nor the sky which is beyond. What stirred? Where? In whose protection? Was there water bottomlessly deep?

(Translation by Wendy O'Flaherty, Penguin Classics Edition, p.25).

p.47 The late Premier of Guyana, Forbes Burnham, was variously known as the Pharoah and the Kabaka. His late sister, even before he came to power, wrote a pamphlet called, 'Beware My Brother Forbes'.